THE HOUSE IN THE SKY

A BAHAMIAN FOLKTALE

RETOLD BY
ROBERT D. SAN SOUCI

PICTURES BY
WIL CLAY

DIAL BOOKS FOR YOUNG READERS · NEW YORK

AUTHOR'S NOTE

The House in the Sky follows the traditional pattern of Bahamian storytellers who "mix and match" such familiar elements as "Mock Sunrise," "The Password," or "The Theft of Butter." In my retelling I have interwoven several such narrative strands as drawn from a variety of primary sources. Among the most helpful were Daniel Crowley's *I Could Talk Old-Story Good: Creativity in Bahamian Folklore,* Elsie C. Parson's *Folk-Tales of Andros Island, Bahamas* and *Folk-Lore from the Cape Verde Islands, Part I,* and Charles L. Edwards's *Bahama Songs and Stories: A Contribution to Folk-Lore.* Other readings provided information on the region's history, culture, and physical setting.

Published by Dial Books for Young Readers
A Division of Penguin Books USA Inc.
375 Hudson Street
New York, New York 10014

Designed by Julie Rauer
Printed in Hong Kong
First Edition
10 9 8 7 6 5 4 3 2 1

Library of Congress Cataloging in Publication Data
San Souci, Robert D.
The house in the sky/by Robert D. San Souci;
pictures by Wil Clay.
p. cm.
Summary: A lazy, greedy brother gets his comeuppance
when he tries to take more than his fair share from a
house full of spirits.
ISBN 0-8037-1284-7.—ISBN 0-8037-1285-5 (lib. bdg.)
[1. Folklore—Caribbean Area.] I. Clay, Wil, ill. II. Title.
PZ8.1.S227Ho 1996 398.21—dc20 [E] 92-39958 CIP AC

The artwork was prepared with acrylic paints on canvas. It was then color-separated and reproduced as red, blue, yellow, and black halftones.

To Alan and Rick,
once again in friendship.
With thanks for your encouragement,
and in hopes that you enjoy this tale
of Boukee and Rabby.

R.S.S.

To my youngest son, Donato.

W.C.

ONCE UPON A TIME, IN THE OLD PEOPLE'S TIME, there were two brothers who lived near each other in shacks at the edge of the jungle. Neither brother liked to work. But Rabby was clever and always got his family plenty of peas and yams and flour and butter. Boukee was greedy, and didn't have much sense. He and his family were always hungry.

Boukee's wife said, "Why don't you go and look for food? You can't give your children nothing to eat. But Rabby always has plenty to eat."

"Well, I gonna ask my bro' where he get all that food," said Boukee.

That evening he stopped Rabby at the jungle's edge and said, "Your family always got something to eat. I never got nothing. How is that?"

Rabby said, "Get up early in the morning, and I'll show you where to find all kind of food."

Boukee said, "All right, Bro'. You come at sunup." He went home to his hungry wife and children and said, "Tomorrow I bring you all the peas and rice and butter I can."

All night Boukee waited for dawn. But his insides were so empty, they grumbled and growled and wouldn't let him sleep. He got up and said, "This night don't look like it ever gonna end. But I can't get no food until my bro' come at sunup."

Then he had the kind of idea that comes to someone with a head as empty as his belly. He went up the hill east of Rabby's house and lit a big old bonfire. He climbed on top of Rabby's roof and shouted, "Co-coo-roo-co!" so his brother would think the rooster was crowing at day-clean.

Rabby leaned out his window and said, "Boukee, what happening?"

"Aren't you ready to go find food?" asked Boukee. "The sun coming up and the rooster been crowing a long time."

"I don't see no sun—just a fire on the hill," said Rabby. "And I didn't hear no rooster. But I sure heard *you*. Bro', you lucky I'm so tired I won't knock you down. Put out that fire and go back to bed. I get you when the sun come up for true."

Rabby closed his shutters with a loud *bang*.

After Boukee put out the fire and went home, he was so tired he fell asleep. He didn't even wake up when his brother came knocking at dawn, so Rabby went into the jungle by himself.

That evening Rabby came back with a sack full of good things to eat. When Boukee saw him, he asked, "Why you didn't come for me at day-clean?"

"I did," Rabby said, "but you wouldn't wake up. I thought you'd rather be sleeping."

"Well, you come for me tomorrow," said Boukee. "I be ready."

All night Boukee watched for the dawn. As quick as the day was clean, he put on his hat, took the biggest sack he could find, and ran to meet his brother.

Then Rabby led him deep into the jungle. All the time Rabby used his machete to *Chop! Chop! Chop!* at the weeds and bushes.

They came to a place where there was just some grass. High up was a big old house sitting on a cloud. While they were looking, the house floated down to the ground. Out of the door came three spirit-folk—a papa, a mama, and a little girl. They were giant size and covered with hair. Their hands had claws and their feet were on backward. Behind them trotted a mean-looking dog with red eyes.

When the spirits went into the woods, the house rose back to the sky.

Rabby said, "There's plenty of food in that house. Those spirits got so much, they never miss any."

"How do we go up there?" Boukee asked.

"I call that house down," said his brother. Then Rabby sang,

Mary, come down so low,
Mary, come down so low,
Mary, come down so low,
Till you touch the ground.

Sure enough, that big old house dropped lower and lower until it sat on the grass. But when Boukee tried to open the door, he found it locked tight.

"How we gonna get in?" Boukee asked.

Rabby said, "Open, *Kabanja*!" and the door opened wide.

The brothers went into the house, and the door slammed shut behind them. Then the house rose back up to the cloud.

Inside they found shelves and cupboards and boxes and barrels filled with food. There was rice, flour, pork, sugar, butter, coffee, peas, coconuts, bananas, star apples, sweet and hot peppers, oranges, papaws, and so much more!

Rabby went to filling his sack with these things. But Boukee was so greedy, he started eating everything he could.

Pretty soon Rabby asked, "Bro', you ready to go?"

Boukee said, "I ain't started filling my sack."

"We got to go," said Rabby, "'fore those spirits get back."

Boukee looked out one of the little windows and said, "I don't see none of them coming. This food is so good, I *got* to fill my belly 'fore I fill my bag."

"Ain't you ashamed to be so greedy?" said his brother.

Boukee just took one mouthful of biscuit and another of potato bread. Then he reached for sweet cakes sitting on the big old stove. These were so hot, he burned his mouth—but he ate them anyway.

"You never *did* have no sense, just greediness," said Rabby. Then he sang softly,

> *Mary, go down so low,*
> *Mary, go down so low,*
> *Mary, go down so low,*
> *Till you touch the ground.*

When the house reached the grass, Rabby said, "Open, *Kabanja*!" and the door opened. He left his brother and went home.

Boukee just kept gobbling down food, while the door snapped shut and the house flew back up to the cloud.

When he couldn't eat any more, Boukee began to feel sleepy. He stretched out on the bed for just a nap, but he slept away most of the day.

Near evening he woke up and said, "I better fill my sack and get home 'fore those spirits find me." He began stuffing his bag with every bit of peas and rice and pork and what-all he could find. When he couldn't cram any more into the sack, he put as much butter as he could under his hat.

Suddenly the house dropped down to the ground. Boukee realized that the spirits had come back. Quick as a wink, he threw the sack of food in a closet and hid himself under the bed.

The hairy spirit-folk came in with their dog. But when the house went back up in the sky, the spirits made their big old dog sit on the cloud outside the door.

The mama and papa spirits put their little girl on the bed that Boukee was hiding under. The papa spirit lit a fire in the stove, and the mama cooked dinner. Then she brought a plate of food to her little girl.

It smelled so good that Boukee, under the bed, got hungry all over again.

He reached up his hand from behind the bed and said, "Give me some. Give me some."

The little girl-spirit always did what she was told. So she gave Boukee some of her food. But this only made him want more. So he kept saying, "Give me some more. Give me some more."

Now the girl's mama started to wonder how such a little child could eat so much. She said, "That's a lot of food you're eating."

"It's for *Me*," the girl said.

"Well, that's all right," her mama said. She gave her another plate heaped with good things to eat.

The girl gave this to greedy Boukee, who kept saying, "Give me some more."

"*Me* wants some more," the little girl said.

"Now, you *can't* have room for no more!" her mama cried.

"It's not for *me* on the bed," the girl told her. "It's for *Me* under the bed."

"Oho!" cried the mama and papa together. They looked under the bed and saw Boukee hiding there. So they dragged him into the kitchen and stood him up alongside the big stove.

"You been thiefing our food?" asked the papa.

"No," said Boukee, "I just come in for a rest. I hide 'cause I got scared you'd think I been thiefing. But I ain't got no food of yours."

Now while he was telling them this, all the butter he hid under his hat melted from the stove heat. It ran down his head and shoulders.

"You been thiefing my butter!" cried the papa. He grabbed Boukee, saying to his wife, "Boil up a pan of water and we'll dash it on this thief!"

But Boukee, covered with butter, twisted out of the spirit's hand. Then he ran around that big old house, looking for a way out. But every time he got near the front door, he forgot the words to make it open. He kept shouting, "Open, *Babanja*!" and "Open, *Dabanja*!"

Then the little girl, who was watching all this, said, "All you got to say is 'Open, *Kabanja*!'"

So Boukee cried, "Open, *Kabanja*!"

The door flew wide open. But the spirit's big old red-eyed dog was waiting outside. He chased after Boukee until Boukee fell right off the edge of the cloud.

Down, down Boukee fell, until he landed in the top of a banana tree.

Buttery and hurting, Boukee climbed down and started for home.

Rabby, sitting on his porch smoking a pipe, saw his brother. He just shook his head and said, "Too greedy."

When Boukee's little boy and girl saw him coming, the butter gleaming in the last rays of sunlight, they shouted, "Pa's here, and he's shining with gold!"

But when Boukee's wife saw him, she made him climb into a tub of hot water. She scrubbed so hard to get the butter off him that he felt he might just as well have stayed in the sky and let the spirits scald him.

Next day Rabby told Boukee, "Those spirits move that house where I can't find it."

"Don't matter," Boukee said. "I been thinking it one bad idea to go thiefing other folks' food."

"Bro', this the first thinking I ever hear from you," said Rabby. "Maybe you right."

Then they started growing their own food. It was hard work, but they always had enough to eat.